P9-CQP-687

Dear Tabby

By
Carolyn Crimi
Illustrated by
David Roberts

HARPER
An Imprint of HarperCollins*Publishers*

For information address HarperCollins Children's Books, a division of HarperCollins Publishers, 10 East 53rd Street, New York, NY 10022.
www.harpercollinschildrens.com

Library of Congress Cataloging-in-Publication Data
Crimi, Carolyn.
Dear Tabby / by Carolyn Crimi ; illustrated by David Roberts. p. cm. — 1st ed.
Summary: A feline advice columnist assists other animals with their problems, such as a parrot whose owners complain that he talks too much, a groundhog who feels the pressure of predicting the weather, and a cat who objects to being pampered.
ISBN 978-0-06-114245-1 (trade bdg.) — ISBN 978-0-06- 114246-8 (lib. bdg.)
[1. Advice columns—Fiction. 2. Animals—Fiction. 3. Humorous stories.] I. Roberts, David, date, ill.
PZ7.C86928 Dea 2010 2007041935
[E]—dc22 CIP
AC

Typography by Carla Weise
11 12 13 14 15 SCP 10 9 8 7 6 5 4 3 2 1 ❖ First Edition

Got Troubles?

Trying to kick the catnip habit?
Itching to ditch those pesky fleas?
Sick of the same old "fetch, roll over, stay" routine?
Tabby D. Cat can help!
Tabby D. Cat has been helping the furry and the feathered for all nine of her lives. Send your letters to:

Tabby D. Cat
Dumpster with the Dented Top
Straye Street Alley
Critterville, IL

Please include payment with your letter. Table scraps welcome.

BOOTS
Boots Whitepaw
78 Drivingmecrazy Drive
Critterville, IL
Dear Tabby,
My owner is a little girl named Emily.
She makes me eat sardines! She read
somewhere that cats like them. Who would
tell lies like that? (Dogs, no doubt.) How
can I get her to feed me what I want?
Best regards,
Boots
P.S. I've enclosed one with this letter.
See how awful they are?!

Dear Boots,

Wish I could help you, my finicky friend, but I'm too busy licking my paws after that delicious sardine. For your information, most cats do like sardines, especially hungry alley cats who don't have kind owners like you do.

Purrfectly yours,

Tabby D. Cat

MANFRED BASSET HOUND
16 SAD STREET
CRITTERVILLE, IL

Dear Tabby,
What is the key to happiness?
I sit on my porch day after day, but
nothing happy ever happens to me.

Mournfully yours,
Manfred

Dear Manfred,

That's a pretty big question! Let me think about it and get back to you. Try chasing your tail while you wait. Seems to work magic on you canine types.

Purrfectly yours,

Tabby D. Cat

Pauline Parrot
16 Chatty Cathy Court
Critterville, IL

Dear Tabby,

My owners keep threatening to give me away because I talk too much. Well, you know, if they wanted a pet who doesn't talk, they should have gotten a snake or a fish or a lizard, because I love to talk and talk and talk and sometimes I do find myself talking too much, but then I remind myself that I am a parrot and we parrots are chatty because what else do we have to do for crying out loud, sit on a pirate's shoulder? I mean, come on, there are no pirates left but if there were I would fly off to be with a pirate and show those owners of mine just how awful it is to be in a quiet house, and I would have plenty of gold coins, too, because pirates have lots of gold coins and they give them to their parrots, I am sure of it. Right?

Pauline

Dear Pauline,

Um, what was the question?

Purrfectly yours,

Tabby D. Cat

-LOST-

One small bear wearing a tutu and riding a bike. Answers to the name of Betty. If found, please call the Dingaling Sisters' Traveling Circus.

Stanky Skunque
22 Lovelorn Lane
Backyard, Lilac Bush
Critterville, IL

Dear Tabby,

I've been lonely for so long. Something about the white stripe down my back puts everyone off. It's sort of hard to meet girls when they're screaming and running away from you. Should I just give up?

Love,

Stanky

Dear Stanky (ever thought about changing your name, by the way?),

Be patient, my fragrant friend! For every saltshaker there's a pepper mill, for every cup there's a saucer, and for every ham there's a cheese. I know that somewhere there's a gal with the good scents—er, sense—to see the beauty of your inner, stripeless self.

In the meantime, try some cologne.

Purrfectly yours,

Tabby D. Cat

Betty Bear
Maple Avenue Park
Critterville, IL

Tabby!

My brother always gets to ride the bike with the new horn. I am always stuck riding the bike with the flashing light. I like the horn better! This is not fair, so I have run away from the Dingaling Sisters' Traveling Circus. Don't try to bring me back, 'cause I won't go. Don't tell my brother that I'm living in the park on Maple Avenue. Don't tell him how dark it gets at night and how the owls are kind of scary. And whatever you do, don't tell him I'm sorry about all the dumb things I said.

Betty

Dear Betty,

I must apologize. A horrible thing has happened to your letter. A gust of wind blew it right out of my paws. I chased it for half a block, but I'm afraid it blew right into the Dingaling Sisters' Traveling Circus. I think I saw your brother reading it. I realize that this is the last thing you wanted to happen!

Again, I am truly sorry.

Purrfectly yours,

Tabby D. Cat

Boots Whitepaw
78 Drivingmecrazy Drive
Critterville, IL
Dear Tabby,
Things have gotten worse. Now Emily
insists on putting me in silly little sweaters.
Some of them are even pink.
I think you'll agree this is a cat-astrophe.
Best regards,
Boots

Dear Boots,

What's wrong with sweaters? Believe me, I could use a sweater on cold nights in the Dumpster. Be thankful you have an owner who keeps you warm.

Purrfectly yours,

Tabby D. Cat

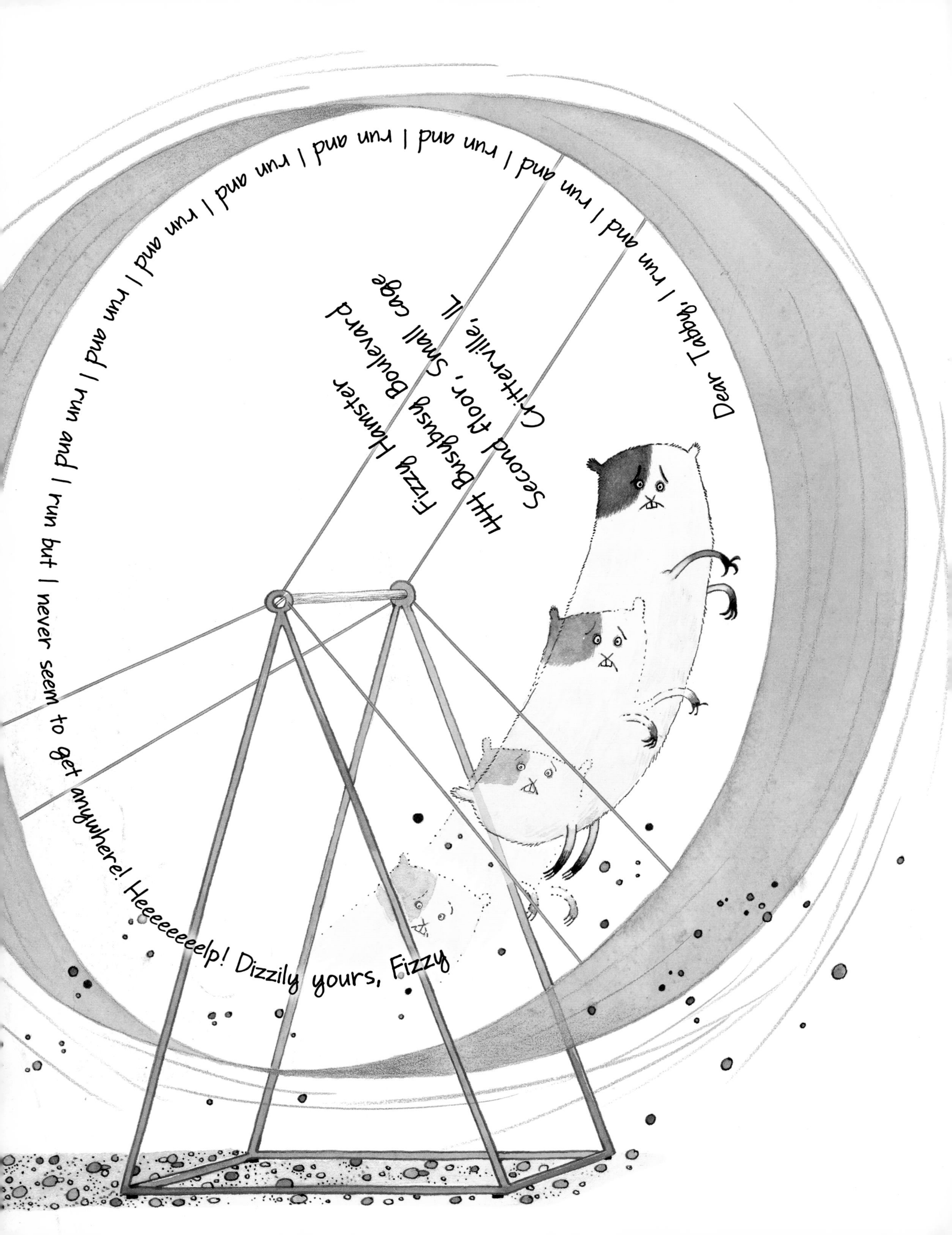
Dear Tabby, I run and I run and I run and I run and I run and I run and I run and I run and I run and I run and I run but I never seem to get anywhere! Heeeeeeeelp! Dizzily yours, Fizzy
Fizzy Hamster
444 Busybusy Boulevard
Second floor, Small cage
Critterville, IL

Dear Fizzy,

Think outside the circle! Get off that wheel before your world spins out of control! Pay attention to the finer things in life, like celery stalks and carrot sticks. Don't forget to stop and smell the cedar chips along the way.

Purrfectly yours,

Tabby D. Cat

Dear Tabby,

I wrote to you before because my owners keep saying that they might give me away or maybe they'll just let me go by throwing me out the window and then I'm not sure what I would do, except that it might be nice to fly up high in the sky with real live wild birds but I wonder if we'd all get along or if they'd try to peck my eyes out or whatever so maybe it's better for me to stay right here in my nice safe house, in which case I should probably learn how not to talk so much. What do you think?

Pauline

Dear Pauline,

True conversation involves both LISTENING <u>and</u> TALKING. If you have a hard time listening, try snacking instead of yakking. Every time you get the urge to babble, pop a cracker into your beak.

Purrfectly yours,

Tabby D. Cat

Boots Whitepaw
78 Drivingmecrazy Drive
Critterville, IL

Dear Tabby,

It's gotten worse.

I put up with the sardines. I put up with the sweaters. I even put up with the Santa hat last Christmas. But now she puts me in a BABY CARRIAGE. She rolls me around town like I'm some kind of doll. Is there no end to my misery? What's a self-respecting cat supposed to do?

Best regards,

Boots

Dear Boots,

A baby carriage is a fine way to get around. I'm stuck with the old-fashioned method—my paws. Sorry, but I still say you're one lucky cat.

Purrfectly yours,

Tabby D. Cat

Guy Groundhogg
Critterville Petting Zoo
Cage Closest to the Hot Dog Stand
Critterville, IL

Dear Tabby,

This is my first Groundhog Day and I'm freaking out, dude! Everyone expects me to tell them when spring's coming! WHY ME? What do I look like, a barometer?

Cracking under pressure—

Guy

Dear Guy,

Take deep, cleansing breaths, my frazzled friend! Just because humans get all worked up about this shadow stuff doesn't mean you have to. News Flash: Winter will end when it wants to whether you see your shadow or not. So just put on your shades and SHINE on your special day!

Purrfectly yours,

Tabby D. Cat

GROUNDHOG WITH GUMPTION!

The town of Critterville watched in awe as the resident groundhog made history on February 2. Normally a mellow fellow, this gutsy guy zipped onto the scene and did a snazzy dance number that residents have since dubbed "The Groundhog Groove."

"I don't know if he saw his shadow or not," said the Critterville zookeeper, "but he sure did look like he was having a good time!"

For Sale:
One used hamster wheel. Best offer.

Pleasantly plump parrot looking for someone to share her perch with. Enjoys crackers, talk shows, and candlelit dinners for two. Bad listeners need not apply.

Stan K. Skunque
and
Louella U. Stinque
Request the Honor of Your Presence
at Their Wedding
This Saturday at 4:00 pm
Nose Plugs Suggested
16

Boots Whitepaw
78 Drivingmecrazy Drive
Critterville, IL

Dear Tabby,

I've tried. Really, I have. But the sweaters, the sardines, the baby carriage—they're just not my style. And now she's started calling me Bootsy-Wootsy-Boo-Boo-Bear. That's it! Time for me to hit the road! I am really a traveling kind of cat anyway. But I'm worried about Emily. She's a sweet kid, and she'll be so sad. Any parting tips?

Best regards,

These **Boots** Are Made for Walkin'

Dear Boots,

Go, my freedom-loving friend. Don't worry about Emily. I've got a plan.

Purrfectly yours,

Tabby

Dear Emily,
Please take care of this cat. She is
clean and kind and will listen to all
your troubles. All she asks for in return
is that you love her back.
Purrfectly yours,
A Friend

Tabby D. Cat
c/o Emily
78 Drivingmecrazy Drive
Critterville, IL

Dear Manfred,

You asked what the key to happiness is. Well, sometimes happiness is right there beside you. You might even be passing it on your daily walk! But a lot of times you have to make happiness happen. Sniff it out, hunt it down, dig dig dig until you find it. Just be sure to get out there and look for it, my forlorn friend! Take it from me, it's there. Good luck!

Purrfectly yours,
Tabby D. Cat